PICKIN' PETER

igloo

Peter picked anything and everything.

He picked his ears, his *tummy* button, his toe nails and, especially, his nose.

It made no difference where he was or what he was doing. Peter always had his finger up his nose.

And when he found a bogey, he secretly stuck it somewhere out of sight!

"For goodness sake, Peter. That's revolting," his mum said. "At least use a hanky."

But it was no use. Peter just kept on picking.

One day, Peter's *mum* was cleaning the living room when she happened to find an unusually large and revolting bogey.

"That's it!" she yelled. "I've had just about enough of this. If I find one more of these horrible things, there'll be no sweets for a month."

Peter decided to escape into the garden. He could feel something bogey-like up his nose and he wanted to investigate.

He sat down under the apple tree, had a quick look round to make sure no one was watching and began to pick away.

Then, still looking round, he stuck the bogey on the tree.

When Peter turned to look at the bogey, he couldn't believe his eyes. There on the tree was the biggest bogey he had ever seen. And it was moving!

"Wow!" he gasped. "It's fantastic!"

He popped the bogey into a matchbox so he could show it to his best friend, Ronnie, when he came round to play.

Peter took Ronnie straight to his room where he had hidden the matchbox.

Ronnie was just as excited as Peter. He loved bogeys, too, and a bogey that moved was something very special indeed.

But, when Peter opened the matchbox, it was empty.

"Oh, no!" cried Peter. "The bogey's escaped! My mum will go mad if she finds it."

The two boys searched high and low.
But the bogey was nowhere to be seen.

Soon, it was lunch time and Ronnie had to go home. Peter sat down at the table.

"Here we are," his *mum* said, as she put two plates of cheese salad on the table. "Eat up, now."

But Peter wasn't hungry. His mind was on the lost bogey. And then he saw it... it was on his mother's plate and... it was eating her lettuce!

Peter jumped up and knocked over his glass of milk. "Never mind," said his *mum* and went off to find a cloth.

As soon as her back was turned, Peter grabbed the bogey and put it in the coffee tin.

After lunch, Peter's mum cleared the table and tidied the tin away. She put it on the very top shelf in the kitchen. Where Peter couldn't reach it.

Several days passed. Peter grew more and more worried. If his mother found the bogey, he'd be in big trouble, and no mistake. In fact, he was so worried, he even stopped picking his nose.

His mum was delighted.

Then, one day, the worst happened...

Peter's *mum* had invited her friends over for coffee. She took down the coffee tin from the top shelf and opened it...

Peter's heart sank.

But something very strange happened. Instead of finding a horrid, green bogey, a beautiful, rainbow-coloured butterfly flew out of the tin and fluttered around the kitchen.

"Isn't it beautiful," said Peter's mum. And all her friends agreed.

"Hmm," thought Peter. "Who'd have thought that a bogey could make my mum so happy. I wonder if there are any more."

And he set off at once to find out.

also available...

Rude Roger   Dirty Dermot   Pickin' Peter   Space Alien Spike   Silly Sydney   Nude Nigel

Shy Sophie   Cute Candy   Royal Rebecca   Grown-up Gabby   Terrible Twins   Show-off Sharon